AN M. NIGHT SHYAMALAN FILM
THE LAST AIRBENDER

THE AVATAR'S RETURN

adapted by Irene Kilpatrick
based on the series *Avatar: The Last Airbender* created by
Michael Dante DiMartino and Bryan Konietzko
based on the screenplay written by M. Night Shyamalan

Simon Spotlight
New York London Toronto Sydney

SIMON SPOTLIGHT

An imprint of Simon & Schuster Children's Publishing Division

1230 Avenue of the Americas, New York, New York 10020

 © 2010 Paramount Pictures. All Rights Reserved. *The Last Airbender* and all related titles, logos, and characters are trademarks of Viacom International Inc.

SIMON SPOTLIGHT and colophon are registered trademarks of Simon & Schuster, Inc.

For information about special discounts for bulk purchases, please contact Simon & Schuster Special Sales at 1-866-506-1949 or business@simonandschuster.com.

Manufactured in the United States of America 0410 LAK

First Edition

10 9 8 7 6 5 4 3 2 1

ISBN 978-1-4169-9939-3

"Hey, something is under there!" said Sokka, kneeling down to look at a patch of glowing ice. He and his sister, Katara, had been hunting tigerseal for their tribe. They were members of the Southern Water Tribe—a tribe that long ago boasted many waterbenders, but now Katara was the only one who could control water.

Unsure of what lay underneath, Katara hit the glowing ice with Sokka's boomerang. Suddenly, a bright light shot into the sky as the ice cracked open to reveal a young boy with a shaved head, and a large furry animal.

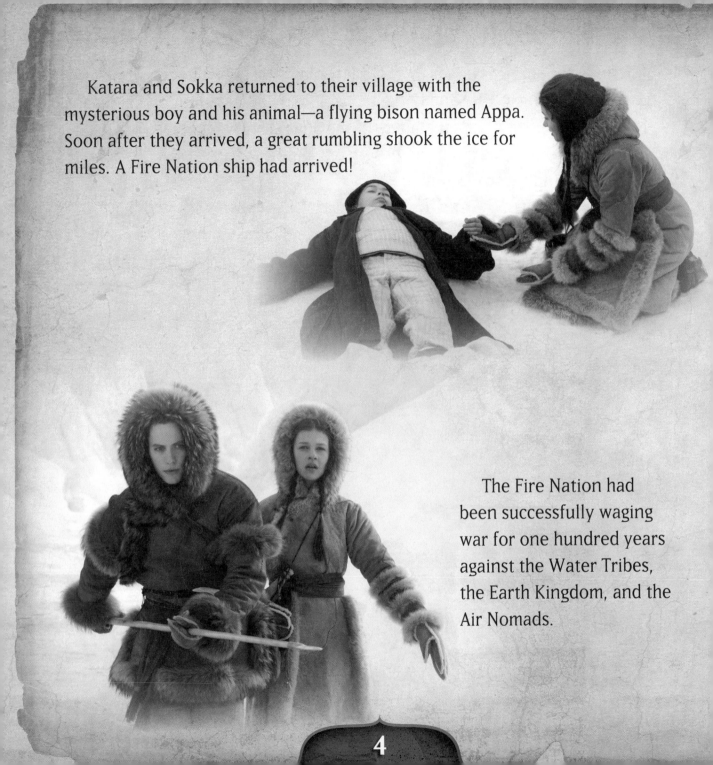

Katara and Sokka returned to their village with the mysterious boy and his animal—a flying bison named Appa. Soon after they arrived, a great rumbling shook the ice for miles. A Fire Nation ship had arrived!

The Fire Nation had been successfully waging war for one hundred years against the Water Tribes, the Earth Kingdom, and the Air Nomads.

A young man with a burn scar on his face led a group of soldiers to the village. Katara and Sokka watched helplessly as the leader entered their igloo and dragged the boy to the ship.

"Why did they take *him*?" asked Sokka.

"I don't know," said Katara. "But we have to save him."

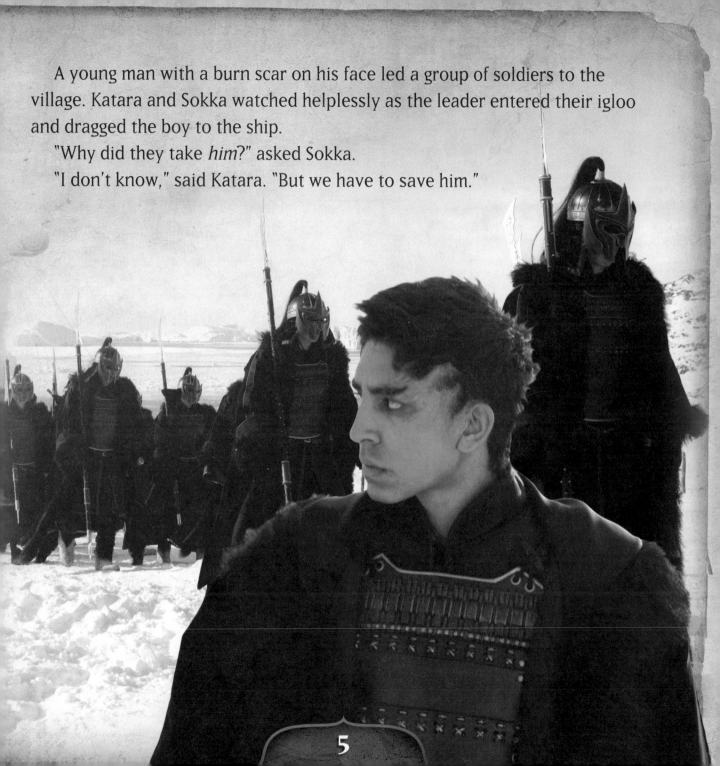

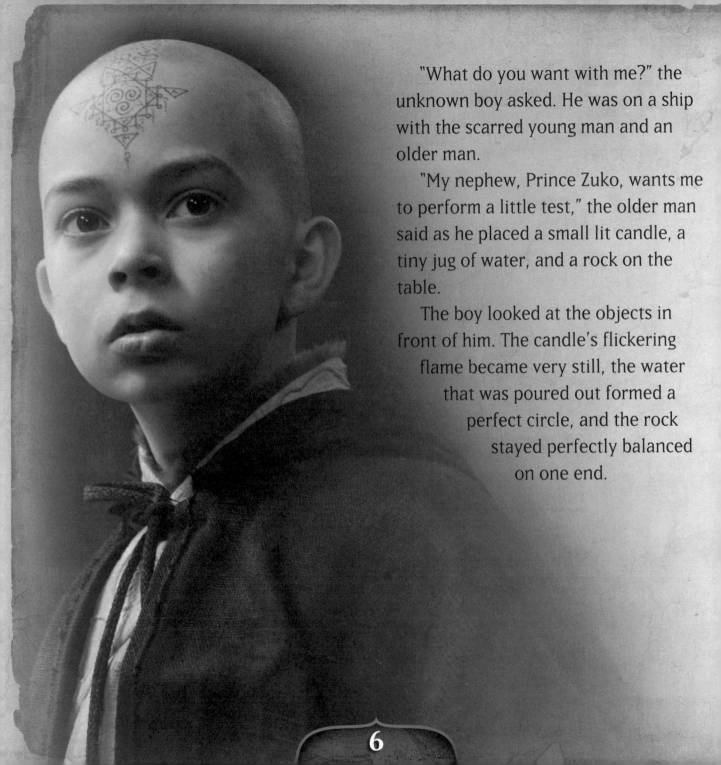

"What do you want with me?" the unknown boy asked. He was on a ship with the scarred young man and an older man.

"My nephew, Prince Zuko, wants me to perform a little test," the older man said as he placed a small lit candle, a tiny jug of water, and a rock on the table.

The boy looked at the objects in front of him. The candle's flickering flame became very still, the water that was poured out formed a perfect circle, and the rock stayed perfectly balanced on one end.

"He can control all the elements!" Prince Zuko exclaimed. "He is the Avatar, Uncle Iroh."

Iroh nodded and then looked at the boy. "You are the only one in the entire world who could pass this test. My nephew has been searching for you a long time. It is truly an honor to be in your presence."

"You are my prisoner, boy," said the prince. "I'm taking you back to my father, the Fire Lord, to restore my honor."

Frightened, the boy lifted his arms and pushed a strong gust of wind toward Iroh and Prince Zuko. It knocked the two men off their feet. He ran out onto the deck of the ship and saw Katara and Sokka waiting for him on top of Appa. He leaped into the air, flipped open his staff, and glided up to meet them.

"Where should we take you?" asked Katara. "Where is your home?"

"The Southern Air Temple," said the young boy.

Prince Zuko ran out and stared up at the sky in disbelief, "I underestimated him, Uncle, because he looked like a boy. I won't do that again."

When the group arrived at the Southern Air Temple, it was deserted. "I don't understand," said the boy. "I left just a few days ago. Where is everyone?"

Katara was beginning to understand what had happened. "Is it okay if you tell me your name?" she asked.

"Aang," he said.

"Aang, I think you were in that ice for almost *a hundred years*," Katara said softly. "The Fire Nation knew the Avatar would be born into the Air Nomads, so . . . you're the Last Airbender in the world."

"You're lying," Aang said, shaking his head.

Overcome with sadness, Aang's body unexpectedly began to float above the ground. His eyes and tattoos started to glow and a great gust of wind surrounded him. Then a bright light filled his mind, and Aang saw that he was in the spirit world. As he walked toward a cave, a big, scaly dragon came out and curled around him.

The Dragon Spirit spoke to Aang: *Avatar. The world is in danger. Go to the Northern Water Tribe, the last stronghold against the Fire Nation. There you will be called upon to save both the human and spirit worlds.*

Aang now knew what he had to do. He opened his eyes and turned to Sokka and Katara, "We have to go north—to the Northern Water Tribe."

Meanwhile, outside the Fire Lord's palace in the Fire Nation, Commander Zhao paced back and forth impatiently. "We are tracking the stories of the Avatar through the towns. There are many sightings of him," he told Fire Lord Ozai.

The Fire Lord frowned. "The Avatar will bring the Fire Nation down—he needs to be stopped."

"My lord, I believe the Avatar will go to the Hall of Avatars at the Northern Air Temple for guidance. Let us set a trap," Commander Zhao replied with a wicked grin.

As the group made their way north, Aang was still unsure of what the Dragon Spirit wanted him to do. How could he save the world from the Fire Nation?

Aang decided to go alone to the Northern Air Temple's prayer room to speak to the Dragon Spirit again. But, as soon as he entered, he was captured by Fire Nation soldiers. Commander Zhao's plan had worked!

While Commander Zhao proudly told the soldiers in the courtyard that he had captured the Avatar, a shadowy, masked figure—the Blue Spirit—opened the prayer room door and released Aang.

The Blue Spirit and Aang fought off the Fire Nation guards together. Just as they reached the outside gates, an arrow whizzed by and knocked the Blue Spirit to the ground. Aang pulled off the mask and gasped. It was Prince Zuko! Aang had to return to the others, but he left Prince Zuko safely hidden.

Aang now knew that he needed to master bending the other elements, so the three friends headed to the last stronghold against the Fire Nation: the Northern Water Tribe.

When they arrived, they were met by the Northern Water Tribe's ruler, Princess Yue, and the tribe's leaders. Aang convinced them that he was the Avatar by showing his tattoos and performing an airbending move. The tribe's leaders welcomed the newcomers and agreed to let Aang and Katara learn waterbending from Master Pakku.

Although Aang had been
training with Katara during
their journey, he still found
water difficult to control. It
was not at all like bending air.

"Water is the element
of change," Master Pakku
told Aang as they practiced.
"To master water, you must
release your emotions and
let them lead you. Let your
emotions flow like water."

Just then black snow began to fall. It could only mean one thing: The Fire Nation had arrived! Aang needed to ask the Dragon Spirit how to defeat the Fire Nation.

"I know a place where the spirits are strong," said Princess Yue. "The city was built around it. We must hurry!"

Aang, Katara, and Sokka followed Princess Yue down a tunnel of ice until they reached a small courtyard with a pool. As the battle began along the outer wall of the fortress, Sokka and the princess returned to the city to join the battle while Aang sat down to meditate. Katara stood to the side, ready to protect him.

The Dragon Spirit spoke to Aang: *Show the Fire Nation the power of water. Remind them that all elements are equal. That is why an Avatar must exist.*

In the meantime, Prince Zuko had secretly stowed away on Commander Zhao's ship. As soon as the ship got close to the frozen fortress walls, Zuko dove into the water and swam under the ice, then broke through the surface with the fiery heat of his hands. He followed Aang's tracks to the courtyard.

Katara fought hard to protect Aang, but Zuko was not going to let him get away again. He fought back with even greater strength and knocked her to the ground. As Katara fell, she saw Zuko carrying Aang back toward the fortress.

Aang remained deep in meditation even as Zuko carried him away from the spiritual place. When he finally awoke, he found himself in a storage room filled with barrels of water.

"It was fun escaping with you from the Air Temple," Aang told Zuko, who was pacing the length of the room. "We could be friends, you know."

"Never," said Zuko as he bent a burst of fire toward Aang. Zuko didn't need friends; he needed his father's forgiveness.

Aang shielded himself with a ball of wind, which made the fire spurt out in all directions. Just then Katara arrived. She put the fires out by using the water from the barrels and finished off by freezing Zuko inside a block of ice.

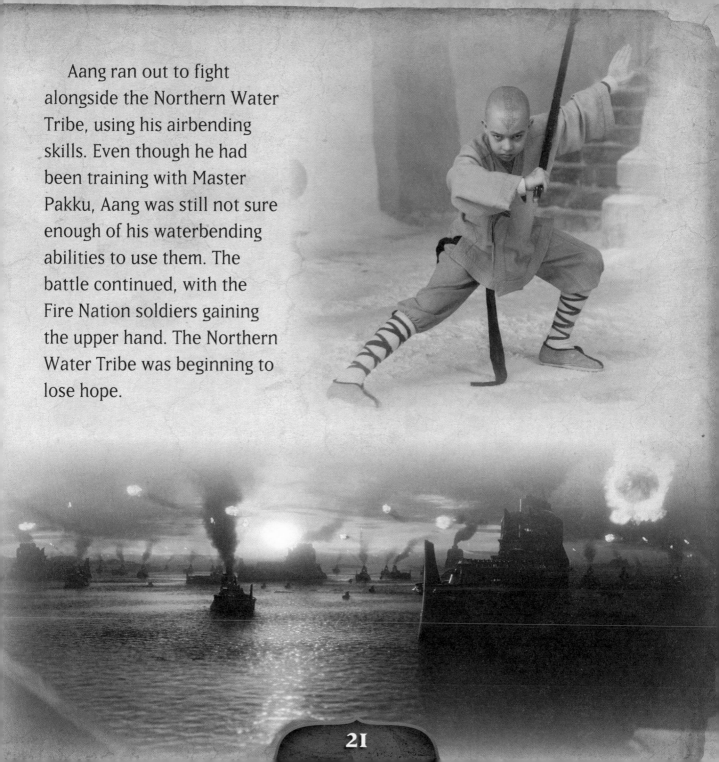

Aang ran out to fight alongside the Northern Water Tribe, using his airbending skills. Even though he had been training with Master Pakku, Aang was still not sure enough of his waterbending abilities to use them. The battle continued, with the Fire Nation soldiers gaining the upper hand. The Northern Water Tribe was beginning to lose hope.

Aang couldn't let them lose. He was the Avatar—the only one who could save them.

He raced to the top of the crumbling fortress wall and faced the Fire Nation ships. Aang thought about the wise words of Master Pakku and the Dragon Spirit. He raised his arms and remembered all of his friends and teachers who were gone, and thought, I am the Last Airbender.

He let his feelings flow throughout his whole body, and he raised his arms even higher.

Soon the ocean waters started to shift and shake, and then a huge wave rose into the air, towering over the walls of the fortress.

Seeing that they were powerless against this great wave of water, the Fire Nation had no choice but to retreat. They raced back to their ships, knowing now that fire was no longer the strongest element.

At sea, a safe distance from the city, Iroh and Prince Zuko sat in a kayak. Zuko had used the warmth of his hands to free himself from Katara's block of ice and had been rescued by his uncle.

"The Avatar has mastered water," said Iroh.

When the last ship had disappeared over the horizon, the overjoyed Northern Water Tribe turned toward Aang and bowed. They were honoring the Avatar, who had truly returned and brought hope with him.

Aang bowed back. He was finally ready to accept that he was the Avatar. And with the help of his new friends, he was going to save the world.